SPECIAL TASK AIRCRAFT

PHYLLIS EMERT

JULIAN  *MESSNER*

For Matthew Brooks Emert

The author wishes to acknowledge the Carruthers Aviation Collection, Sprague Library, Harvey Mudd College, Claremont, California, and express thanks to Nancy R. Waldman, Librarian, Sprague Library, for her help and cooperation in preparation of the *Wild Wings* series.

Lib. ed. 10 9 8 7 6 5 4 3 2 1
Paper ed. 10 9 8 7 6 5 4 3 2 1

Library of Congress Cataloging-in-Publication Data

Emert, Phyllis Raybin.
    Special task aircraft / Phyllis Emert.
        p.   cm. – (Wild wings)
    Includes bibliographical references.
    Summary: Describes the specifications and uses of various airplanes designed for specific tasks, including the Northrop YB-49 Flying Wing, Aero Spacelines Super Guppy, and Bell/ Boeing V-22 Osprey.
    1. Airplanes–Juvenile literature.   [1. Airplanes.]   I. Title.
II. Series: Emert, Phyllis Raybin.   Wild wings.
TL547.E48   1990
629.133'34–dc20
    ISBN 0-671-68963-0 (lib. bdg.)   ISBN 0-671-68968-1 (pbk.)
                                                        90-31488
                                                            CIP
                                                            AC

Photo credits and acknowledgments

Pages 6, 9, 38, 41, 54, and 57 courtesy of Experimental Aircraft
Pages 10 and 13 courtesy of Northrop
Pages 14 and 17 courtesy of Hughes
Page 26 courtesy of North American/Rockwell
Pages 22, 25, 34, and 37 courtesy of Lockheed
Pages 42 and 45 courtesy of Grumman
Pages 58 and 61 courtesy of Boeing

CONTENTS

INTRODUCTION

Throughout aviation history, airplanes have been designed and built for special jobs. As the need for a certain aircraft grew, planes were developed to fill that demand.

The need for ocean patrols during World War II led to the development of military seaplanes, called "flyingboats."

The importance of gathering information and photographs among the superpowers made it necessary to design and build advanced reconnaissance "spyplanes."

When rocket parts in the space program became so large that no aircraft could carry them, giant airplanes were built just for this purpose.

Experimental rocket planes broke the barriers of speed and altitude, gaining valuable information for the design of future supersonic planes and spacecraft.

New challenges in the skies have been met by the development of advanced, and sometimes unusually designed, aircraft.

In the past, progress in aviation has kept pace with the demands placed on it, and it should continue to do so in the future.

CONSOLIDATED-VULTEE PBY CATALINA

1930s—1960s

SPECIFICATIONS

ENGINE:
Number: 2
Manufacturer: Pratt and Whitney
Model: R-1830-92
Rating: 1,200 horsepower each

ACCOMMODATIONS:
10 or more passengers when used as a rescue plane

FIREPOWER:
2 .50-caliber machine guns in nose-mounted ball turret, two .30-caliber guns on sides of hull behind wings, and four 500-pound bombs or 450-pound depth charges fitted under wings

DIMENSIONS:
Wingspan: 104 feet
Length: 63 feet, 10 inches
Height: 18 feet, 10 inches

OTHER INFORMATION:
Manufacturer: Consolidated-Vultee (now Convair)
Crew: Up to 9
Maximum Takeoff Weight: 34,000 pounds
Ceiling: 18,200 feet
Maximum Range: 3,100 miles
Maximum Speed: 196 miles per hour

The Consolidated-Vultee PBY Catalina was one of the most successful flying boats ever built. First flown in 1935, it became famous for its ability to take a lot of punishment and tackle even the most difficult of missions.

With a range of over 3,000 miles, the Catalina was often used for patrol and tracking duties during World War II. Crews would scan large areas of the Pacific Ocean for signs of enemy ships, submarines, or aircraft, and radio their positions back to base.

Some Catalinas launched torpedoes or strafed enemy positions, while others carried bombs and depth charges. PBYs inflicted great damage on the enemy. One pilot was credited with sinking 20 Japanese ships and damaging 46 others!

Flying at speeds of up to 196 miles per hour, PBY flying boats were still slower than enemy fighter planes and open to attack. Although armed with several machine guns, the seaplane crews had difficulty defending themselves against the faster, more maneuverable Japanese Zeros. But many of the tough Catalinas took direct hits and kept on flying.

PBYs saw combat action with English and Canadian forces but the United States Navy used them mainly in air-sea rescue missions. For downed flyers, the Catalina was the difference between life and certain death.

A typical mission might start with an important radio message from headquarters. "We've got a B-25 bomber crew in the drink waiting for pick-up. There's heavy anti-aircraft fire, so take along some fighters."

Two P-38 Lightnings escorted the PBY Catalina as it flew to the downed crew's last reported position.

"Attention Black Cat [a Navy nickname for the Catalina]. We've spotted the crew below. There's heavy flak

from onshore guns. You make your pick-up and we'll keep the bad guys busy."

As the flying boat landed in the sea, the P-38s strafed enemy gun positions. Nine B-25 crew members, several of them with injuries, were plucked from the water. Some were clinging to debris from the remains of their bomber. Others had on life jackets.

Once they were all onboard, the Catalina wasted little time. It took off from the choppy sea and headed for home.

"We've got some hull damage after that rough landing," reported the copilot. "Hold on, I just spotted another one of our boys below."

"I see him," said the Catalina. "We're going back in. Get ready for another bumpy ride."

The damaged Catalina landed again to rescue still another flyer before finally returning to base.

PBY production stopped in 1945, but after the war many countries continued to use them as transports and rescue craft into the 1960s. Some were converted to water-scoopers and used as flying fire-engines, dumping lake water on fast-moving forest blazes.

NORTHROP YB-49 FLYING WING

1940s — 1950s

SPECIFICATIONS

ENGINE:
Number: 8
Manufacturer: General Electric
Model: Y-35-A-5 turbojets
Rating: 4,000 pounds of thrust each

FIREPOWER:
20 .50-caliber machine guns in 4 outer-wing-mounted turrets and tail cluster, and an assortment of bombs, rockets, and missiles

DIMENSIONS:
Wingspan: 172 feet
Length: 53 feet, 1 inch
Height: 15 feet

OTHER INFORMATION:
Manufacturer: Northrop
Crew: 6
Maximum Takeoff Weight: Over 200,000 pounds
Ceiling: 40,000 feet
Maximum Range: About 4,000 miles, depending on payload
Maximum Speed: 520 miles per hour

Jack Northrop believed that an all-wing aircraft could fly faster, farther, and more efficiently than one with wings, a fuselage, and a tail. He built the first true flying wing in 1940. It was called the N-1M.

One year after the United States declared war on Japan in 1941, the XB-35 Flying Wing was designed by Northrop for the Air Force. It was to be a long-range bomber which could fly nonstop from America to Germany and back. The four-engine aircraft would have a range of 10,000 miles without refueling, and a top speed of 240 miles per hour.

But by the time the XB-35 was built and made its first flight in 1946, the war was already over. A long-distance bomber wasn't needed since Germany was defeated.

In 1947, Northrop built a jet-powered version of the Flying Wing called the YB-49. Powered by eight General Electric engines, the sleek, 172-foot, all-wing airplane had a range of 4,000 miles and a maximum speed of 520 miles per hour.

During 1948 and 1949, the YB-49 set many new speed and distance records. One flew from Muroc (now Edwards) Air Force Base in California to Andrews Air Force Base in Washington, D.C. It was a distance of 2,258 miles and the YB-49 flew it in 4 hours and 25 minutes at a speed of 511 miles per hour.

The Flying Wing was competing against Consolidated-Vultee's B-36 to be the main strategic bomber of the United States Air Force. The winner would receive a large government contract.

According to Jack Northrop, the Secretary of the Air Force, Stuart Symington, wanted Northrop to merge with Consolidated. When Northrop refused, the Air Force cancelled its order for the Flying Wing. Instead, Consolidated

was given the contract to build B-36 bombers.

The Air Force said it cancelled because of a shortage of funds. By 1952, they had junked all YB-49s that were left until not a trace of the project existed. Not even a museum had one on exhibit. The Northrop Flying Wing "slipped into history," and Jack Northrop resigned from the company.

One of the interesting characteristics of the YB-49 was that it was nearly invisible on radar screens. This was proven when a test pilot flew one into the San Francisco Bay area from hundreds of miles at sea. The plane wasn't detected on radar until it was almost directly overhead. The advantage of such a plane was that it could fly into enemy territory undetected. Yet this didn't matter to the Air Force at the time. Today, more than 40 years later, this type of design is called Stealth technology. And Northrop's B-2 Stealth bomber of 1990 is remarkably similar to the Flying Wing of 1947!

Jack Northrop, a man clearly ahead of his time, once said, "To focus on the wings is to be on the side of the birds in their seemingly effortless flight—to be on the side of the angels."

HUGHES HK-1 HERCULES—
THE "SPRUCE GOOSE"
1940s

SPECIFICATIONS

ENGINE:
Number: 8
Manufacturer: Pratt and Whitney
Model: R-4360-4A
Rating: 3,000 horsepower each

ACCOMMODATIONS:
Up to 700 fully equipped combat troops

DIMENSIONS:
Wingspan: 319 feet, 11 inches
Length: 218 feet, 8 inches
Height: 49 feet, 6 inches (to top of tail)

OTHER INFORMATION:
Manufacturer: Hughes
Crew: 18
Maximum Takeoff Weight: 400,000 pounds
Ceiling: 17,400 to 20,900 feet, depending on payload
Maximum Range: 3,500 miles
Maximum Speed: 235 miles per hour

The Hughes HK-1 Hercules was the largest airplane in the world when it was first built in the 1940s. Nicknamed "The Spruce Goose," the giant Hughes flying boat was powered by eight Pratt and Whitney engines with a total of 24,000 horsepower.

Construction began in 1942 during World War II. Millionaire Howard Hughes, with shipbuilder Henry Kaiser, set out to design a huge aircraft able to transport 700 combat troops across the Atlantic Ocean to the war in Europe.

The world's largest building was constructed in Culver City, California, to house the big plane's parts. The HK-1 was made entirely of wood treated with a special resin to make it hard and strong.

The fuselage, wings, and tail were built separately from each other. The fuselage was 165,000 cubic feet in size. The inside height of each wing, where it attached to the main body, was 11½ feet. The tail was taller than an eight-story building. The eight propellers were each over 17 feet in diameter.

The war ended in 1945 but construction on the flying boat continued. In June 1946 the separate parts were moved 28 miles to Terminal Island near Long Beach Harbor. The parts were so big that electric and telephone wires had to be cut. Traffic stopped as the giant fuselage, wings, and tail were driven by. The move took five days and crowds lined the streets to watch "the world's largest airplane" go by.

Final assembly took months. Finally, on November 2, 1947, the completed HK-1 made several test runs at Long Beach Harbor. With Hughes as the pilot and dozens of reporters and radio announcers on board, the plane traveled in the water at speeds of up to 90 miles per hour.

"We won't fly her today," Hughes told his guests. "The

water is too choppy."

Most of the press left the HK-1 before its last run of the day. One who stayed aboard was James McNamara of KLAC radio in Los Angeles.

"I'm speaking to you from the flight deck of the Howard Hughes 200-ton flying boat," he broadcast. "We're in Long Beach Harbor making the last test run of the day. This mighty monster of the skies is up to 50 miles per hour now. Fifty over a choppy sea. Fifty-five. More throttle. Sixty. Sixty-five now. Seventy..."

Suddenly everything was very quiet in the cockpit. The giant plane had lifted off the water into the air!

"We're airborne! The plane is in the air. We're flying!" The HK-1 flew 85 feet above the water for nearly one mile. It reached a speed of over 100 miles per hour. But it never flew again.

The Spruce Goose stayed at Pier E on Terminal Island until 1982. Then it was moved to a large dome next to the Queen Mary in Long Beach. Now open for public viewing, the Spruce Goose has been called "a monument to man's never-ending fascination with flight."

BELL X-1
Late 1940s

SPECIFICATIONS

ENGINE:
Number: 1
Manufacturer: Reaction (ree-AK-shun) Motors
Model: Experimental rocket with 4 cylinders
Rating: Up to 6,000 pounds of thrust

DIMENSIONS:
Wingspan: 28 feet
Length: 31 feet
Height: 10 feet, 10 inches

OTHER INFORMATION:
Manufacturer: Bell
Crew: 1
Maximum Takeoff Weight: 13,400 pounds
Ceiling: More than 70,000 feet
Maximum Range: Does not apply
Maximum Speed: About 1,000 miles per hour

The Bell X-1 was the first airplane to fly faster than the speed of sound. Above 40,000 feet, sound travels at 660 miles per hour. This is called Mach 1. The X-1, piloted by Chuck Yeager of the United States Air Force, flew at Mach 1.06 (about 700 miles per hour) on October 14, 1947.

The X-1 was a small bullet-shaped aircraft painted bright orange. It was 31 feet long and had a wingspan of 28 feet. Its straight wings were strong but thin, only three and a half inches at the thickest point.

This experimental plane was powered by a rocket divided into four cylinders. These cylinders could be fired one at a time or together for a total of 6,000 pounds of thrust. Liquid oxygen and alcohol fueled the rocket engine mounted in the tail.

A small hatch cover was the only way out of the cockpit. In case of trouble, the pilot could dive out of the hatch, but the thin sharp wings made this very dangerous.

This "flying bullet with wings" carried over 8,000 pounds of rocket fuel, more than twice its own weight. But the X-1 used up its entire supply of fuel after just a few minutes of flight.

To save fuel, the small airplane was carried to a high altitude under the fuselage of a B-29 Superfortress. Then it was ready to try for the first supersonic flight ever.

"Ready, Yeager?" asked the B-29 pilot, Bob Cardenas, over the intercom.

"Let's get it over with," Yeager replied. Cardenas began counting down from ten.

Many believed the X-1 would break apart at Mach 1 because of the powerful shock waves that airplanes encounter at high speeds.

"Three, two, one, drop," said Cardenas. The X-1 fell free of the B-29. Yeager fired all four rocket cylinders, one after

the other, and began to climb.

"I'm at .88 Mach," he reported. "There's heavy shock waves. Leveling off. I'm at .96 Mach. The ride is smooth now."

Suddenly the Mach needle started moving wildly. "I must be seeing things," Yeager declared in disbelief. "The Machmeter is acting screwy. It just went off the scale at .965 Mach!"

Down on the ground the tracking van cut in. "We just heard a sonic boom, like a rumble of thunder!" The loud noise was caused by shock waves at the speed of sound bouncing off the airplane.

Yeager had broken the sound barrier! For 20 seconds he flew the X-1 at 1.07 Mach!

A few months later Yeager flew the small rocket plane at nearly 1,000 miles per hour (Mach 1.45). For more than two and a half years the X-1 was used as a flying laboratory, making tests and gathering information at supersonic speeds.

In 1950 it was retired from service and is now on display at the Smithsonian Institution in Washington, D.C.

LOCKHEED U-2
Mid-1950s—1970s

SPECIFICATIONS

ENGINE:
Number: 1
Manufacturer: Pratt and Whitney
Model: J57C or J75-P-13 turbojet
Rating: 11,000 or 17,000 pounds of thrust

DIMENSIONS:
Wingspan: 80 feet
Length: 49 feet, 7 inches
Height: Information not available

OTHER INFORMATION:
Manufacturer: Lockheed
Crew: 1
Maximum Takeoff Weight: 17,270 pounds
Ceiling: Over 70,000 feet
Maximum Range: More than 3,000 miles
Maximum Speed: More than 500 miles per hour

The Lockheed U-2 was a long-range high-altitude photo-reconnaissance aircraft. First flown in 1955, it was secretly developed to take pictures and gather information useful to the United States about other countries.

Although some U-2s were used to collect weather information about air turbulence, cloud formations, and the jet stream, its main purpose was reconnaissance. This became public in May of 1960, when Air Force Pilot Gary Powers was shot down in his U-2 airplane over the Soviet Union while flying a secret mission. From then on the press referred to the U-2 as a "spyplane." Powers was imprisoned in the Soviet Union for two years before his release in 1962.

The United States didn't believe that the Soviets had the radar and missile capability to bring down such a high-altitude plane. After the Powers incident, the government cancelled any further flights over the USSR.

U-2s played a central role in the Cuban Missile Crisis of 1962. U-2 photos showed Soviet ships delivering missiles to Cuba. Other pictures confirmed the building of sites with missiles aimed at the United States.

President John F. Kennedy blockaded Cuba and demanded that the Soviets remove the missiles. During a tense week, the two superpowers seemed at the edge of war. It was the Russians who gave in first and withdrew their missiles under the watchful cameras of high-altitude U-2 aircraft.

The U-2, which had one Pratt and Whitney turbojet engine, was actually a powered sailplane with an 80-foot tapered wingspan. The range of this lightweight plane could be extended by shutting off the engine and gliding.

The U-2 had a unique landing gear. Its twin main wheels and small twin tail wheels pulled forward and up

into the fuselage. Small wheels under the outer wings dropped away as the wing gained lift during the takeoff. Turned-down wing tips were used as skids (in place of wheels) during landings.

The U-2 flew more than 500 miles per hour at an altitude of 70,000 to 80,000 feet. Although the cockpit was pressurized, the pilot wore a lightweight full-pressure suit in case of a bail-out at such high altitudes.

NASA (National Aeronautics and Space Administration) used U-2 airplanes in carrying out experiments in astronomy and physics. U-2s were also used to map the entire state of Arizona and even collect debris from the 1980 Mount St. Helens volcanic explosion in Washington state.

NORTH AMERICAN X-15

Late 1950s–1960s

SPECIFICATIONS

ENGINE:
Number: 1
Manufacturer: Reaction Motors
Model: XLR99-RM-2 rocket
Rating: 70,000 pounds of thrust

DIMENSIONS:
Wingspan: 22 feet
Length: 52 feet, 5 inches
Height: 13 feet, 6 inches

OTHER INFORMATION:
Manufacturer: North American
Crew: 1
Maximum Takeoff Weight: 50,914 pounds
Ceiling: 354,200 feet
Maximum Range: Does not apply
Maximum Speed: 4,534 miles per hour

The North American X-15 experimental research plane reached speeds and altitudes greater than any other aircraft flying within the earth's atmosphere. This hypersonic (at least five times the speed of sound) rocket aircraft flew between 1959 and 1968. The flight test results of the X-15 contributed to the development of future space vehicles and other high-speed airplanes.

The X-15 had short, tiny, straight wings with a span of only 22 feet, and a long, tubelike fuselage. Its lower tail fin was jettisoned (thrown off) before landing so it didn't scrape on the ground. The landing gear consisted of two nosewheels and twin steel skids under the rear fuselage.

The X-15 was mostly made of titanium and stainless steel to withstand temperatures as high as 1200 degrees Fahrenheit at high altitudes. It was also coated with an "armor skin" of nickel alloy steel and other heat-resistant material. During high-temperature test flights, some sections of the X-15 became hot enough to turn bright red.

The X-15 was powered by a Reaction Motors rocket engine which used 10,000 pounds of fuel per minute. The aircraft carried 18,000 pounds of fuel. A later version carried outside tanks that held another 13,000 pounds and were jettisoned when empty.

Each of the 199 test flights of the X-15 lasted from 84 to about 180 seconds. That's how long it took for the powerful rocket engine to empty the fuel tanks. The rocket plane would then glide to a landing at Edwards Air Force Base in California, where all the testing was done.

The X-15 had to be air-launched at high altitudes (about 40,000 feet) to conserve fuel. A Boeing B-52 Stratofortress acted as the mother ship and carried the smaller plane beneath its wing. Once the desired altitude was reached, the X-15 was set loose from the B-52 and the

test pilot fired the engine.

Only three experimental planes were built and tested during the nine-year program. In 1967, one of the X-15s reached Mach 6.72, which is equivalent to 4,534 miles per hour! Another flew to an altitude of 354,200 feet. That's 67 miles straight up!

Those records are still unmatched by any other aircraft. X-15 pilots flew so high that they received astronauts' "wings" by traveling more than 50 miles above the earth.

At these extremely high altitudes, the air was so thin that the X-15 was difficult to control. Twelve small rockets were installed in the wingtips and nose of the plane. To move right, a left wing-tip rocket was fired. To move up, a lower nose rocket was fired down, and so on. These small rocket thrusters were the basis for similar controls in later manned spaceflights.

When the X-15 program ended in 1968, one of the planes went to the United States Air Force Museum. The other went on display at the National Air and Space Museum, in Washington, D.C. The third was lost in a crash in 1967.

AERO SPACELINES SUPER GUPPY

Mid-1960s–1970s

SPECIFICATIONS

ENGINE:
Number: 4
Manufacturer: Pratt and Whitney
Model: T34-P-7WA turboprops
Rating: 7,000 horsepower each

ACCOMMODATIONS:
41,000-pound payload including the third stage (section) of the Saturn V launch vehicle and the Apollo Lunar Module Adapter

DIMENSIONS:
Wingspan: 156 feet, 3 inches
Length: 141 feet, 3 inches
Height: 46 feet, 5 inches

OTHER INFORMATION:
Manufacturer: Aero Spacelines
Crew: 6 or more
Maximum Takeoff Weight: 175,000 pounds
Ceiling: 20,000 feet
Maximum Range: About 3,000 miles
Maximum Speed: Over 300 miles per hour

The Aero Spacelines Super Guppy was built to carry the giant booster rockets in America's space program. Flown for the first time in 1965, the Super Guppy was constructed from parts of a Boeing transport plane.

The United States was committed to putting a man on the moon and bringing him back again in the 1960s. This lunar project was called Apollo. A giant booster rocket, the Saturn V, was developed in three sections (called stages) to power the Apollo spacecraft out of the earth's atmosphere and through 240,000 miles of space.

This booster rocket was as high as a 36-story building and weighed more than a Navy destroyer. It had a diameter of 33 feet and a height of 363 feet. Three large moving vans could be driven, side-by-side, into the fuel tanks of the first stage alone!

The manufacturing and testing of the Saturn V booster rockets took place in Alabama, Mississippi, Louisiana, and California. Then the rockets had to be transported to the Kennedy Space Center in Florida where launches took place; they were so large that NASA had to float them by barge down the Mississippi River across the Gulf of Mexico and by ship through the Panama Canal.

No airplane then in existence was big enough to carry these giant parts. Aero Spacelines enlarged a Boeing B-377 Stratocruiser and called it the "Pregnant Guppy." They lengthened the rear fuselage and added a large bubble section on the top.

But an even larger aircraft was needed which could accommodate the third section of the Saturn V and the Apollo Lunar Module Adapter. (The Lunar Module was the small craft the astronauts used to transport themselves to the moon's surface from the Command Module).

The Super Guppy was built for this purpose. It used the

wing, flight deck, and forward fuselage of a Boeing C-97 J transport. The huge transport had a hinged nose section which lifted up and allowed for straight-in loading of oversized cargo.

Called the world's ugliest airplane, the Super Guppy had a large bubble-type top fuselage, a length of 141 feet, 3 inches and a wingspan of 156 feet, 3 inches. The cargo compartment had a volume of 49,790 cubic feet. It was over 108 feet long, 25 feet wide, and 25½ feet high.

The lunar project reached its goal with Apollo 11 on July 16, 1969. Neil Armstrong became the first human to set foot on the surface of the moon.

A commercial version of the Super Guppy was also built. It was used to carry oversized McDonnell-Douglas DC-10 airliner fuselage parts and Lockheed L-1011 airliner wings.

LOCKHEED SR-71 BLACKBIRD
1960s –1980s

SPECIFICATIONS

ENGINE:
Number: 2
Manufacturer: Pratt and Whitney
Model: J58 turbojets
Rating: 32,500 pounds of thrust each

DIMENSIONS:
Wingspan: 55 feet, 7 inches
Length: 107 feet, 5 inches
Height: 18 feet, 6 inches

OTHER INFORMATION:
Manufacturer: Lockheed
Crew: 2
Maximum Takeoff Weight: 170,000 pounds
Ceiling: Over 80,000 feet
Maximum Range: Over 15,000 miles
Maximum Speed: More than 2,000 miles per hour

The Lockheed SR-71 Blackbird was a long-range photographic and electronic reconnaissance aircraft. It gathered information, surveyed land areas, and examined weapon and troop movements of other countries. First operated in 1964, the SR-71 was capable of flying worldwide at high altitudes and supersonic speeds of over 3,000 feet per second!

The Blackbird (actually dark blue, not black, in color) was regularly improved and updated. It was equipped with the most advanced sensor electronics and surveillance (observation) systems available, much of which were kept secret.

The SR-71 was powered by two Pratt and Whitney J58 turbojets, each developing 32,500 pounds of thrust (forward force). They allowed the Blackbird to reach speeds over 2,000 miles per hour at altitudes of more than 80,000 feet.

The long, thin fuselage and 56-foot delta-wing were made of titanium and its alloys (mixtures of metals). This heat-resistant metal withstood temperature changes while operating at different speeds and altitudes.

During refueling at subsonic speeds, the temperature of the plane's skin could drop as low as 90 degrees below zero Fahrenheit. At supersonic speed, it could rise to hundreds of degrees above zero. The wheels and tires of the launching gear were protected from the heat by being placed deep within the fuselage fuel tanks.

The pilot and reconnaissance systems officer (RSO) sat in separate cockpits, one in front of the other. The RSO's duties included those of a copilot, flight engineer, and navigator.

Both cockpits were fully pressurized, heated, and air-conditioned. Crew members wore special gravity suits in

case they had to eject from the plane. The ejection escape system was designed to operate successfully at ground level and up to speeds of more than Mach 3 at 10,000 feet.

The SR-71 carried a wide variety of advanced observation equipment. Its multi-sensor high performance systems could survey 60,000 square miles in one hour from an altitude of 80,000 feet. Advanced photographic sensors were located in the front portions of the wing and body.

In 1974, one SR-71 flew the 3,500 miles from New York to London in one hour and 55 minutes. Then it returned nonstop from London to Los Angeles, about 6,500 miles, in 3 hours and 48 minutes. In 1976, another Blackbird reached a straight-line speed of 2,193 miles per hour, which was a world aircraft record.

Before Defense Department funding cuts in late 1989, the SR-71 Blackbird was the world's fastest, highest-flying plane in service.

AEROSPATIALE/BRITISH AIRCRAFT CORPORATION CONCORDE

Late 1960s –1980s and beyond

SPECIFICATIONS

ENGINE:
Number: 4
Manufacturer: Rolls Royce/SNECMA
Model: Olympus 593 Mk 610 turbojets
Rating: 38,050 pounds of thrust each

ACCOMMODATIONS:
Up to a maximum of 144 passengers, depending upon seating arrangements (Air France and British Airways operate with a single-class layout of 100 passengers)

DIMENSIONS:
Wingspan: 83 feet, 10 inches
Length: 203 feet, 9 inches
Height: 37 feet, 5 inches

OTHER INFORMATION:
Manufacturer: Aerospatiale/British Aircraft Corporation
Crew: 3, plus 6 cabin attendants
Maximum Takeoff Weight: 408,000 pounds
Ceiling: 60,000 feet
Maximum Range: About 4,000 miles, depending on load
Maximum Speed: More than 1,300 miles per hour

The Aerospatiale/British Aircraft Corporation (BAC) Concorde was the world's first supersonic transport airliner in commercial service. The Concorde was developed and produced by Great Britain and France after the two countries entered into a joint agreement in 1962.

First flown in 1969, the Concorde began regular service in 1976 with British Airways and Air France. The sleek, beautiful airplane looks like a giant bird with a long neck and drooping nose. The nose is lowered during takeoffs and landings to allow for better pilot visibility. It extends straight out at speeds above 290 miles per hour.

The 70-degree swept-back wing gives the plane a dartlike appearance. Its slender, delta-shaped design produces maximum lift and helps the Concorde achieve speeds of Mach 2. This is twice the speed of sound, more than 1,300 miles per hour!

An aircraft flying faster than the speed of sound produces sonic booms. These are shock waves that make a loud booming sound heard on the ground. The Concorde has a distinct double boom and because of this, several countries, including the United States, have banned supersonic flight over populated areas.

A typical flight begins with a message from the airport control tower. "Concorde 173, cleared for takeoff," declares the air traffic controller at Heathrow Airport in London, England.

The long birdlike plane starts down the runway, building up speed. The pilot slowly brings the throttles back and the aircraft climbs. The nose is raised and the Concorde increases its speed to just below Mach 1.

Once the plane clears land and is over the Atlantic Ocean, Heathrow gives clearance to climb and accelerate. The Concorde climbs to between 50,000 and

60,000 feet.

"Full power," orders the pilot. He watches the gauges carefully. "Mach 1, 1.5, Mach 2."

The Concorde travels one mile every 2.7 seconds, or 23 miles a minute! The passengers are served coffee and drinks. The ride is so smooth that a full cup sits on a lap tray without a ripple. Lunch is served 11 miles up in an aircraft traveling faster than a rifle bullet leaving its barrel.

Soon the pilot begins reducing speed and descending to a lower altitude. The plane must be below Mach 1 before it crosses the United States coastline.

By the time Concorde approaches Kennedy Airport in New York City, the nose is lowered and the speed is down to 127 miles per hour. Within minutes the plane touches down.

From London to New York, a distance of 3,500 miles, it has taken the Concorde only three and a half hours!

GRUMMAN E-2C HAWKEYE

1970s—1980s and beyond

SPECIFICATIONS

ENGINE:
Number: 2
Manufacturer: Allison
Model: T56-A-427 turboprops
Rating: 4,910 horsepower each

DIMENSIONS:
Wingspan: 80 feet, 7 inches
Length: 57 feet, 7 inches
Height: 18 feet, 4 inches

OTHER INFORMATION:
Manufacturer: Grumman (GRUH-mun)
Crew: 5
Maximum Takeoff Weight: 51,933 pounds
Ceiling: 31,000 feet
Maximum Range: 1,605 miles
Maximum Speed: 372 miles per hour

The Grumman E-2C Hawkeye is an early-warning aircraft used by the United States Navy. It detects and identifies approaching high-speed enemy airplanes. First flown in 1972, the E-2C is equipped with the most advanced avionics systems available today.

The Hawkeye is an unusual-looking airplane. The tail unit has four fins and three rudders. A large saucer-shaped dome is mounted above the rear fuselage. This is the rotodome antenna radar system. It is twenty-four feet in diameter and revolves in flight.

The Hawkeye's radar systems can detect and identify approaching aircraft up to 300 miles away. Each E-2C can automatically track over 2,000 targets. It can control more than 40 airborne intercept missions at one time. A special search radar system can pick up targets as small as a single missile from as far away as 167 miles. This system also monitors enemy ships and land vehicles.

The Hawkeye is powered by two Allison turboprop engines and has a wingspan of more than 80 feet. The flight crew of five includes the pilot, copilot, combat information center officer, air control officer, and radar operator.

Teams of Hawkeyes typically patrol certain naval task force defense areas. Many are assigned to aircraft carriers in trouble spots throughout the world, such as the Mediterranean Sea.

"This is Hawkeye Two to Carrier *Saratoga*. We are picking up three aircraft of unknown origin flying at Mach 1.2 in a northeasterly course."

"Begin automatic tracking, Hawkeye. We will alert our fighters and intercept on your signal."

The Hawkeye's radar detector processor (RDP) automatically tracks the planes and signals target reports to the Combat Information Center officer.

"They could be Libyan planes...no, we have positive identification. They are Saudi planes...and they are now changing course and heading southwest. *Saratoga*, they are friendly aircraft. Cancel alert."

Had they been enemy aircraft flying in the direction of the naval task force, fighters from the aircraft carrier would have been ordered into the air to intercept the planes. If they refused to change course and appeared to be threatening American ships or aircraft, the fighters would then take aggressive action against them.

E-2C Hawkeyes monitor air traffic around Cape Canaveral in Florida during space shuttle launches. They're used by the Coast Guard and Customs Service in intercepting drug-smuggling aircraft. The armed forces of Israel, Japan, Egypt, and Singapore also operate E-2C Hawkeyes.

MacCREADY GOSSAMER
ALBATROSS

Late 1970s

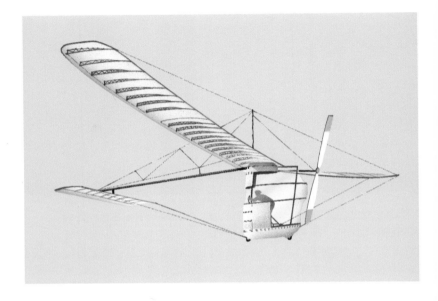

SPECIFICATIONS

ENGINE:
None

DIMENSIONS:
Wingspan: 93 feet, 10 inches
Length: About 32 feet
Height: About 17 feet

OTHER INFORMATION:
Designer and Manufacturer: Paul D. MacCready, Jr.
Crew: 1
Weight: 70 pounds
Takeoff Weight with Pilot: 215 pounds
Altitude: From 6 inches to 25 feet
Speed: Up to 15 miles per hour

The MacCready Gossamer Albatross was the first human-powered aircraft to cross the English Channel. It was made almost entirely of plastic, with a frame of carbon-fiber-reinforced tubing.

The giant wing of the Albatross was 93 feet, 10 inches long, supported by Styrofoam "ribs" and steel wire bracing. DuPont Mylar, a clear polyester plastic film, was used for the wing covering.

The pilot sat in a Mylar-enclosed cockpit, 10 feet high and eight feet long. The canard, which controlled the directions and movement of the aircraft, was located in front of the wing and pilot. Power was created when the pilot pedalled a bicycle without wheels which connected to a drive shaft and propeller. The wing gave the Albatross lift and the propeller gave it forward motion.

A prize of 100,000 pounds (about $300,000) was offered by Sir Henry Kremer for the first human-powered flight across the English Channel from England to France. Twenty-six-year-old Bryan Allen was the pilot of the Albatross when it made its historic flight on June 12, 1979.

At 5:51 A.M. he lifted off from Folkestone, England, and set a course for France. Allen kept the craft steady, eight to 10 feet above the water. After an hour the two-way radio stopped working. He heard the crew but he couldn't answer back.

Suddenly, the Albatross headed into rough air and it quickly dropped close to the water.

"Watch your altitude, Bryan!" warned a crewman. "Bring it up higher. You're down to one foot!"

The small waves of the Channel lapped at the fuselage. Allen had trouble with the headwinds. His strength was gone.

"Keep pedaling, Bryan. Bring it up higher."

But it was no use. He signaled to ditch the flight. He wanted a tow from one of the support boats below. Using his last bit of energy, he pedaled furiously to get height, so a boat could get underneath the aircraft.

Miraculously, at 15 feet, the air was much smoother. Soon his strength returned and he signaled that he would keep going.

Mile by mile, the Albatross crossed the Channel at speeds of up to 15 miles per hour. But it wasn't easy. The height and speed indicators stopped working. The cockpit covering fogged up. Allen's calves and thighs cramped, and he ran out of water.

The final test was flying over the offshore rocks before landing on the beach. Exhausted and in pain, Allen thought of crashing into them but he managed to fly above the jagged barrier.

At last he stopped pedaling. The 70-pound craft that looked like a giant dragonfly landed gently on the sands of France.

The flight of the Gossamer Albatross took two hours and 49 minutes over a straight-line distance of 23 miles.

McDONNELL DOUGLAS KC-10A EXTENDER

1980s and beyond

SPECIFICATIONS

ENGINE:
Number: 3
Manufacturer: General Electric
Model: CF6-50C2 turbofans
Rating: 52,500 pounds of thrust each

ACCOMMODATIONS:
Seating for support personnel at forward end of main cabin, aerial refueling station with seating and large observation windows for boom operator at back end of lower fuselage, cargo payload of up to 169,370 pounds, and fuel payload of up to 200,000 pounds

DIMENSIONS:
Wingspan: 165 feet, 4½ inches
Length: 181 feet, 7 inches
Height: 58 feet, 1 inch

OTHER INFORMATION:
Manufacturer: McDonnell Douglas
Crew: 4 or more
Maximum Takeoff Weight: 590,000 pounds
Ceiling: About 33,400 feet
Maximum Range: About 4,400 miles with full load
Maximum Speed: About 564 miles per hour

The McDonnell Douglas KC-10A Extender is an Advanced Tanker Cargo Aircraft (ATCA). This giant tanker supports the airlift fleet of the United States Air Force Strategic Air Command (SAC). It is capable of refueling Military Airlift Command (MAC) aircraft and transporting troops and supplies anywhere in the world should the need arise.

First flown in 1980, the KC-10A is larger, more efficient, and less costly than KC-135 military tankers, many of which are still used today. It would take 40 KC-135s to fuel an entire F-4 fighter squadron and carry personnel and equipment to the Middle East. Only 17 KC-10As would be needed to do the same job!

Powered by three General Electric turbofan engines, the KC-10A measures over 181 feet long, with a wingspan of 165 feet, 4½ inches. KC-10As are converted McDonnell Douglas DC-10 30CF commercial freighter planes. Extra fuel compartments, a refueling boom and equipment, and military avionics systems (radar, navigation, and communication) are added to the basic airframe of the DC-10.

The refueling boom is the long pole or beam which extends from the tanker plane and connects to the aircraft to be refueled while both are in midflight. The fuel is delivered through the boom to the receiving plane's fuel tanks.

The KC-10A can deliver 200,000 pounds of fuel to other aircraft, 2,200 miles from its home base, and use its own fuel system to return to base.

A fly-by-wire computer system controls the flight of the big tanker and makes adjustments automatically to

maintain speed, course, and altitude during the refueling. The Extender also provides navigation and communications services for aircraft it refuels.

The boom operator is in charge of the refueling mission and sits in the lower rear fuselage area. A large window and periscope observation system let the operator guide the boom so it can connect in flight to other aircraft. Once the boom connections are made, the fuel is transferred from one plane to another at a rate of 1,500 gallons a minute.

United States Navy and Marine Corps aircraft, North American Treaty Organization (NATO) airplanes, and older types of fighter planes still in use are all serviced by KC-10A tankers.

VOYAGER
Mid-1980s

SPECIFICATIONS

ENGINE:
Number: 2
Manufacturer: Teledyne (TEL-e-dyn) Continental
Model: Front/0-240 piston   Back/10L-200 piston
Rating: Front/130 horsepower   Back/110 horsepower

DIMENSIONS:
Wingspan: 110 feet, 9½ inches
Length: 25 feet, 4¾ inches
Height: 10 feet, 3½ inches

OTHER INFORMATION:
Manufacturer: Voyager Aircraft
Crew: 2
Maximum Takeoff Weight: About 10,000 pounds
Ceiling: 20,000 feet
Maximum Range: About 28,000 miles
Maximum Speed: More than 122 miles per hour

Voyager was the first and only aircraft to make a non-stop flight around the world without refueling.

Voyager looked more like a catamaran, a boat with two parallel (side-by-side) hulls, than an airplane. Two long booms intersected the wings. Between the booms was the canoe-shaped fuselage where the small cockpit/cabin area was located.

The engines and propellers were mounted in the front and back of the fuselage. The basic structure of *Voyager* was a honeycomb of resin-treated paper, surrounded by two layers of carbon fiber cloth. The cloth was coated with a hard, strong epoxy covering.

Voyager was designed as one large fuel tank. Sixteen tanks were placed in the more than 110-foot wingspan and fed into the main fuselage fuel tank. The fuselage tank then fed fuel directly to the two Teledyne Continental piston engines through the use of mechanical pumps.

The *Voyager* crew, Dick Rutan and Jeana Yeager, were careful when drawing fuel to keep the weight in the wings evenly distributed. The wings were very flexible. In normal flight, they'd bend up and down 15 feet or more.

The entire length of the cabin/cockpit areas was only seven and a half feet long and two feet wide. Dick and Jeana had to live in this nonpressurized space for more than a week.

The flight began early on the morning of December 14, 1986. *Voyager* took off from Edwards Air Force Base in California and headed west. Onboard was a navigation computer, an autopilot, weather radar, and a long-range radio for communications.

Voyager flew out over the Pacific Ocean past Hawaii. On day three, the autopilot suddenly failed. The trip might have ended right then had it not been for the back-up

unit they brought along, which Jeana installed.

As *Voyager* headed over Africa on days four and five, it met up with bad weather and towering mountains. It climbed to 20,000 feet to get past these barriers.

On day eight, they crossed over Costa Rica and now flew over the Pacific Ocean. By day nine, they had engine trouble and wondered whether there was enough fuel to get back.

Finally, they saw the coast of California. At 8:05 A.M. on December 23, 1986, *Voyager* landed at Edwards Air Force Base. The nearly 27,000 mile trip had taken nine days, three minutes, and 44 seconds. When it landed, there were 18.3 gallons left in the fuel tanks, enough for 800 more miles.

Voyager is on display at the National Air and Space Museum in Washington, D.C.

BELL/BOEING V-22 OSPREY

Late 1980s and beyond

SPECIFICATIONS

ENGINE:
Number: 2
Manufacturer: Allison
Model: T406-AD-400 turboshafts
Rating: 6,150 horsepower each

ACCOMMODATIONS:
• Up to 24 combat-equipped troops,
> or
• Up to 12 stretcher patients plus medical attendants
> or
• Cargo up to 20,000 pounds inside cabin and
  10,000–15,000 pounds on underfuselage hooks

DIMENSIONS:
Wingspan: 46 feet
Number of Rotors: 2
Diameter of Each Rotor: 38 feet
Length: 62 feet, 7½ inches
Height: 20 feet, 10 inches

OTHER INFORMATION:
Manufacturer: Bell/Boeing (BOH-ing)
Crew: 3 or more
Maximum Takeoff Weight: 60,500 pounds
Ceiling: 26,000 feet
Maximum Range: 1,382 miles, depending on payload, as a helicopter; over 2,000 miles, depending on payload, as an airplane
Maximum Speed: More than 115 miles per hour as a helicopter; 345 miles per hour as an airplane

The Bell/Boeing V-22 Osprey is a multimission tilt-rotor vertical lift aircraft. First flown in 1988, it can fly like a helicopter and also like an airplane.

The Osprey, named after the large brown and white hawk, can take off from almost any small area, straight up into the air. For this vertical take-off, its two three-blade rotors are in an upright position. As a helicopter, the Osprey flies at about 115 miles per hour and can hover in the air in one place.

Once airborne, the V-22 has the ability to fly forward like an airplane at much greater speeds than a helicopter. The rotors tilt forward and become propellers, allowing the Osprey to reach speeds of up to 345 miles per hour.

Six V-22 Ospreys are being thoroughly tested today by Bell and Boeing. Once the testing program is completed, the Defense Department will make the final decision whether the aircraft will be funded for large-scale production.

The United States Navy, Marines, and Air Force are all interested in different versions of the V-22 Osprey for use in the 1990s and beyond.

The Marine Corps wants to use it as a troop and support transport to eventually replace its current Sea Stallion helicopters. This model would carry 24 combat-equipped Marines, or an equal amount of cargo, and be able to land on water as well as land.

The Navy wants the Osprey as a combat search and rescue aircraft. They also plan to use it for antisubmarine warfare duties with special radar and sonar equipment and antishipping missiles.

Both Navy and Marine Corps models would operate from ships. Therefore, the wing and rotor systems must fold

up quickly for easy stowage. The Air Force version of the V-22 Osprey would carry 12 special forces troops and equipment over long-range distances.

Powered by two Allison turboshaft engines, the V-22 has a full-width rear loading door and ramp in the underside of the fuselage. It's also equipped with the most modern avionics systems available today, including special night vision, helmet display, and flight control systems.

GLOSSARY

Aggressive—Ambitious, bold, pushy; starting fights or arguments.

Alloys—A mixture of two or more metals.

Antenna—A wire or set of wires used in sending and receiving electromagnetic waves.

Antiaircraft—Defense against enemy airplanes.

Autopilot—An automatic control which flies an airplane by itself.

Avionics—Aviation electronics.

Bail out—To make a parachute jump from an aircraft.

Bank—A sloping turn in an aircraft.

Barge—A large, flat-bottomed boat for carrying heavy freight.

Blockade—To cut off or isolate a particular area.

Boom—A projecting beam on an airplane which connects the tail rotor to the main body.

Booster—A device which increases power and thrust in the launching rocket of a spacecraft.

Brace—To strengthen by propping up or supporting the weight.

Caliber—The diameter of a bullet; the inside diameter of the gun barrel.

Canard—An airplane which has its main controls in front of the wing.

Catamaran—A boat with twin parallel hulls.

Ceiling—The maximum altitude at which aircraft should normally fly.

Cockpit—The place where the pilot and copilot sit in an aircraft.

Commercial—Profit-making.

Cylinder—An enclosed chamber where force is exerted in an engine.

Debris—The remains of something destroyed.

Delta-wing—A triangular-shaped wing on an airplane.

Dome—A rounded roof or covering.

Drive shaft—The bar which transmits motion and power to the mechanical parts of an engine.

DuPont Mylar—A clear polyester plastic material.

Efficient—Working or acting satisfactorily without waste.

Electronics—The science that deals with the behavior of electrons in vacuums and gases, and with the use of vacuum tubes, transistors, and other advanced equipment.

Epoxy—A resin used in surface coatings; noted for its toughness.

Fahrenheit—Temperature scale on which the boiling point of water is 212 degrees, and the freezing point is 32 degrees.

Flak—Bursts of fire from antiaircraft guns on the ground.

Friction—The rubbing of one thing against the surface of another.

Fuselage—The main body of the aircraft.

Hatch—A door or opening in an airplane.

Honeycomb—A structure full of holes similar to the cells made by bees.

62

Horsepower—A unit for measuring the power of an engine.

Hover—To stay in midair in one place.

Hull—The frame or main body of a ship or aircraft that can land on water.

Hypersonic—Traveling at a speed equal to or greater than five times the speed of sound.

Jettison—To throw away.

Lunar—Related to the moon.

Mach 1—The speed of sound; 660 miles per hour above 40,000 feet.

NASA—National Aeronautics and Space Administration.

Navigation—The method of determining position, course, and distance traveled.

Payload—The bomb or cargo load of an aircraft.

Periscope—An instrument through which one can see things reflected by a mirror at the other end.

Piston engine—An engine powered by pistons; pistons are solid metal pieces in the cylinder moved by a rod which is connected to the crankshaft; the movement of the pistons is sent on to the crankshaft.

Pressurized—To keep a normal atmospheric pressure inside an airplane at high altitudes.

Propeller—A rotating shaft fitted with angled blades which provides thrust in air and moves an airplane forward.

Radar—A device that determines location and distance of objects by using ultra-high frequency radio waves.

Range—A specific distance that an airplane can travel on 1 tank of fuel.

Reconnaissance—The art of obtaining information about an enemy area; a survey or examination.

Resin—A substance that comes from plants and trees which is used in plastics, coverings, and coatings to make them harder.

Rotor—The revolving parts of a motor.

Rudder—A device used to steer the aircraft.

Sensor—A device that responds to heat, light, or motion and then triggers a control.

Skid—A runner used in place of a wheel on an aircraft landing gear.

Sonar—Used in detecting submarines; transmits high-frequency sound waves in water and registers vibrations reflected back from an object.

Sonic boom—A loud noise caused by shock waves bouncing off an airplane travelling at the speed of sound.

Squadron—A unit of military flight formation.

Stealth—A way of designing an airplane so it doesn't show up on radar.

Stowage—The storage of things or goods.

Strafe—To attack with machine-gun fire from low-flying aircraft.

Strategic bombing—Continuous bombing attacks on enemy population centers and industry, which destroy their ability to continue fighting.

Subsonic—Less than the speed of sound, which is 660 miles per hour above 40,000 feet.

Supersonic—Faster than the speed of sound, which is 660 miles per hour above 40,000 feet.

Surveillance—A close watch kept over a person, thing, or group.

Taper—To gradually decrease in width or thickness.

Throttle—The valve in an engine which regulates the amount of fuel entering the cylinders.

Titanium—A hard, gray metal which resists corrosion (being worn away).

Turbine—An engine driven by the pressure of steam, water, or air against the curved blades of a wheel or set of wheels.

Turbofan—A fan driven by a turbine in a ducted fan jet engine.

Turbojet—A jet engine in which the energy of the jet operates a turbine, which in turn operates an air compressor.

Turboprop—A jet engine which operates a turbine, which in turn drives the propellers.

Turboshaft—A jet engine that uses the blast of expanding gases to spin a turbine, which in turn cranks a powershaft.

Turbulence—Agitated or disturbed air which causes a bumpy, rough ride in an airplane.

Turret—A clear, Plexiglas half-globe on an airplane in which guns are mounted.